To Burt, who loved this story
—R-M. P.

To my daughters, Louise and Marion, and a special thank-you to Judy Sue
—B. P.

Henry Holt and Company, LLC, *Publishers since 1866*
115 West 18th Street, New York, New York 10011

Henry Holt is a registered trademark of Henry Holt and Company, LLC
Text copyright © 2001 by Rose-Marie Provencher
Illustrations copyright © 2001 by Bernadette Pons
All rights reserved.
Published in Canada by Fitzhenry & Whiteside Ltd.,
195 Allstate Parkway, Markham, Ontario L3R 4T8.

Library of Congress Cataloging-in-Publication Data
Provencher, Rose-Marie.
Mouse cleaning / Rose-Marie Provencher; illustrated by Bernadette Pons.
Summary: Grandma Twilly cannot find the motivation to get her
house cleaned, until she discovers a mouse in her house.
[1. House cleaning—Fiction. 2. Mice—Fiction.]
I. Fudym, Bernadette Pons, ill. II. Title.
PZ7.P94556Mo 2001 [E]—dc21 00-25734

ISBN 0-8050-6240-8
First Edition—2001
Printed in the United States of America on acid-free paper. ∞
1 3 5 7 9 10 8 6 4 2
The artist used watercolor on Lanaquarelle paper
to create the illustrations for this book.

MOUSE CLEANING

Rose-Marie Provencher
illustrated by Bernadette Pons

HENRY HOLT AND COMPANY
NEW YORK

Grandma Twilly took off her flowered apron and plopped into her rocking chair. "What will I do?" she worried aloud as she rocked. "It's past time for spring cleaning and all I want to do is sit and rock."

Squeak-rock, squeak-rock went the rocking chair. A frown puckered Grandma Twilly's brow. For the first time ever, she could not get herself started.

"What will I do?" worried Grandma Twilly again as she stood up to think. Grandma Twilly liked her house to shine. And she knew houses did not get shiny clean from rocking.

Grandma Twilly tried not to look at her dusty desk. She kept her eyes from seeing the spatter spots on her kitchen floor. She tried not to think of her cluttered closets. She sat down again to rock some more.

Faster and faster rocked Grandma Twilly. *Squeak-rock, squeak-rock* went the rocking chair. But when Grandma Twilly stopped rocking, the squeak did not stop squeaking. Instead, *squeak squeak* sounded a teensy-weensy squeak.

With a leap and a screech, Grandma Twilly landed on top of her table.

"There's a mouse in my house! There's a mouse in my house! And one thing I won't have is a mouse in my house!" she cried. Then she knelt on the table to peek underneath. (But she did not see the squeakity mouse, because it was hiding in . . . *the broom.*)

"I will sweep that mouse out of my house," declared Grandma Twilly, climbing off the table. And sweep she did—all day long. But though she swept every floor and every corner, not one peek of that squeakity mouse did she get. (Because it was hiding in . . . *the oven*.)

That night, when Grandma Twilly went to bed, she said, "I have swept that mouse out of my house."

The next morning Grandma Twilly found tiny nibbles in the bread loaf she had tucked away in the oven.

"There's a mouse in my house! There's a mouse in my house! And one thing I won't have is a mouse in my house!" cried Grandma Twilly. "I will scrub that mouse out of my house." And scrub she did. (But she did not see the mouse, because it was hiding in . . . *the sugar bowl.*)

That afternoon as Grandma Twilly walked to the store, she made up a tune in her head and sang it as she strolled along.

"A mousie came to visit me. It thought that it would stay. My sweeping and my scrubbing have sent it on its way."

But when she returned home and opened a drawer, she found a little pile of chewed paper. The beginning of a mouse nest . . .

"There's a mouse in my house! There's a mouse in my house! And one thing I won't have is a mouse in my house!" cried Grandma Twilly louder than ever.

"I will tidy that mouse out of my house," declared Grandma Twilly. And tidy she did. Every drawer and every closet, even the small one under the stairs. (But still, she did not see the mouse, because it was hiding in . . . *an old boot.*)

No sooner had she finished tidying her cluttered closets than Grandma Twilly discovered a tiny trail of mouse-prints in the dust behind the books.

"There's a mouse in my house! There's a mouse in my house! And one thing I won't have is a mouse in my house!" Grandma Twilly shouted so loudly the squeakity mouse held its paws over its ears.

"I will dust that mouse out of my house," cried Grandma Twilly. And dust she did. She dusted high and low and around things and even in things. (Again, she did not see the mouse, because it was hiding in . . . *the cracker box.*)

Grandma Twilly sat in her rocking chair. "I have tried to chase that mouse out of my house. I have swept. I have scrubbed. I have tidied. I have dusted," she said with a sigh.

"GOODNESS ME!"

Grandma Twilly stopped her rocking. "I have done my spring cleaning! From top to bottom, my house is shiny clean!"

Grandma Twilly's laughter filled the room. "That mouse does not know it helped me, but it did. Without that mouse in my house I would not have done my spring cleaning."

And late that night, when the mouse came out of its house behind the striking clock, it found the nicest thank-you dinner it could imagine.

There were crumbles of cheese and sweet icing from a cupcake, a fresh crust of buttered bread, a bit of crispy bacon, and—nicest of all—a pretty dish of raspberry pudding with slices of banana. The mouse's favorite! Grandma Twilly even left a small pink card by the thank-you treats. The card read:

Thank you, mouse.
Because of you,
I cleaned my house!

In the morning, when Grandma Twilly found the mouse dinner gone, even the last jiggly bit of raspberry pudding, she sang: "There's a mouse in my house, there's a mouse in my house. But one thing I don't mind is THIS MOUSE in my house, because it helped me get my spring cleaning done." (But Grandma Twilly did not see the mouse, because it was hiding in . . . *her apron pocket!*)